# ADVENTURES OF ONE UP MAX

## Runic and The Crystal Cave

By

Lisa Shawver

# Adventures of One Up Max Runic and the Crystal Cave

Printed in the United States of America
First Printing: October 2018

Published by: Paradigm Impact
Hello@ParadigmImpact.com


ISBN: 978-0-9977072-2-9

# Table of Contents

# CHAPTER 1

## ONE WEIRD DUDE

M ax gobbled his breakfast down then went to lay by the back door. Just as he snuggled into his spot, ready to take his morning nap, he heard a loud sound.

SWOOOOOOCCCCCCHHHHH.

A blinding flash of light streaked across the yard.

Max jumped up. His blonde ears flew up into the air, even his floppy one. "Huh? Wha—what was that?!" He stood alert with his nose pressed against the glass looking this way and that way. Nothing. "I know I saw something. Where is it?" he wondered out loud.

3

He pressed his nose closer to the glass and tried to sniff. "UGH." He shook his head. "That's not going to work. I gotta get out there."

Max went in search of Mom.

Up the stairs, he flew. He looked in every room. But, Mom wasn't there.

BARK. BARK. BARK.

He flew back down the stairs and looked in every room. No, Mom.

BARK. BARK. BARK.

"Where is she?! Last I saw she went up to get dressed."

BARK. BARK. BARK.

"MAX! What are you barking about?

Do you have to go out?"

"Well, I've been barking my 'out' bark. YES. I want to go out. I gotta get in that yard. You should have seen what I saw. I don't know what it is, but it's sure strange. A bright light flashed by. I gotta get out there and investigate. Let me out, PLEASE."

"Okay, Maxie Man. Come on."

Max walked on Mom's heels. "You can move the pace up there, Mom. Whatever it is might get away."

Mom opened the back door, and Max shot out into the yard. "Thanks, Mom," he yelled.

Hunting high and low, Max sniffed under every bush and around every tree. He sniffed every blade of grass. He sniffed everywhere.

"Ah, there you are, you little scoundrel." Max was on to the scent.

SNIFF. SNIFF. SNIFF.

A glimmer of blue dashed out from behind the barbeque. Max was hot on its trail.

"Hey, stop! I'm not going to hurt you. I promise. I just have to see what you are."

The little critter made a mad dash and squeezed between two chairs. Max sniffed and barked. Then he sniffed and barked some more.

"Hmm. You don't look like a cat or a dog. And, you sure aren't a skunk or a possum. What the heck are you? Hey, do you have scales?"

Max pushed his nose as far as he could get it between the chairs. "Ouch!"

Whatever it was, the little creature bit him.

"Hey, what'd you do that for? I'm not gonna hurt you. I just want to play."

Two yellowish eyes peeked out from in between the chairs. Max backed away. "Don't worry little fella. Look, I'm moving back. It's safe for you to come out."

"MAX!" called Mom, holding the screen door open. "Come on, boy."

In a flash, the little critter drew his head in safely between the chairs. Max couldn't see him any longer.

"NO! Don't be afraid. It's just my mom." Max tried to ease the creature's fear. Turning to Mom, Max cried, "Stop yelling! You're scaring him!"

But, all Mom heard was bark, bark, bark. "Max, do you want to come in?" she yelled.

Max turned to give Mom his "I-want-to-stay-out" look.

WHISSSSH.

Max flipped around. He saw something streak across the yard. "Man, that little guy is fast." He looked at Mom and shook his head. "Thanks, Mom. I finally had him where I wanted him. Now he's gone again."

Mom shrugged her shoulders and chuckled. "Okay, stay outside." She went back inside.

# CHAPTER 2

## THROUGH THE TUNNEL

With Max occupied, the little critter jetted into the field behind the yard. Max raced after him. He ran and ran and ran. Just when he was about to catch up to it, the air turned icy cold and looked wavy. Max stood staring at what seemed to be a hole in the air. *It's like looking through water*, he thought. He shook his head fast, then stared at the hole again. *It really is some kind of crazy wavy hole.*

The critter jumped into the rippling air and disappeared.

"Oh, no you don't." Max hopped right in after him. "Uh, oh. What the heck is this?" Everything was black except for swirling colorful lights all around him. He twirled and whirled as he zoomed through a long tunnel. "Oh, boy, this isn't good." He squeezed his eyes tight. *I wish I didn't follow that stupid critter. I wish I didn't follow that stupid critter. I wish I didn't follow that stupid critter.*

That's all Max could think of. He hoped wishing hard enough would take him home again. It didn't work.

It seemed Max swirled around in the *tunnel thing* forever. Then finally, he could see light through his eyelids. He rocketed toward an opening and blasted out on the other side with a MASSIVE SWOOOOOCCCCCHHHHH. And, with just as massive a PLOP, he landed right on his head. "Ouch...again."

Max sat for a moment, getting his senses back. He got up and shook himself off. He sure wasn't in his backyard anymore. Instead, he was surrounded by purplish-gray rolling hills and mountains. The trees were different shades of blue. In the far, far distance, he could see what looked like the very tops of dark red and orange trees.

Max sniffed the air. Nothing smelled familiar, nothing except the scent of that little rascal.

GAUK. BUAK. GAUK. BUAK.

SCREECCCCHHHH.

GAUK. BUAK. GUAK. BUAK.

GULP. "What's that?" Max ducked his head. "Whatever it is, it sounds big. And, it sounds mean."

Max couldn't remember a time he'd ever shaken with fear, but he was shaking now. "How'd I get here? What am I going to do? MOMMMMMMMM! I WANT TO COME IN NOW!"

Max shook himself forcefully. "Okay, knock it off. You're a big guy. You can handle this. You need a plan, and the first thing on that plan is to find your way back."

With his nose to the ground, Max tried to sniff his way home. He hadn't gone very far so that *holey air thing* had to be around somewhere. He walked this way then that way. He walked around and around in circles.

"This is crazy. Where can it be? I've got to find it." Max searched a while longer. Finally, he gave up. "Okay, that didn't work. Now for number two on my list. OH, WAIT A MINUTE. I didn't list anything else. Okay, next is to find that troublesome critter." Max shook his body again. "Get control of yourself, Max."

Max sat down hard. His nose crinkled like he might cry. He sniffed hard to fight back any tears. "Okay, the new next on your list is to find that troublesome critter." Max's one ear slowly lifted. "Oh, boy, this isn't good. I'm talking to myself now."

Max sniffed the air and latched onto the critter's scent. With his nose back to the ground, he followed it. He went over big rocks, through hollow logs, around bushes and trees, and hill after hill after hill. "How could that little guy get so far so fast?"

Max walked all day. "I just can't walk anymore," he whispered. He found a patch of grass near a big tree and sprawled out. He watched as night crept its way over the land. And, Max did another thing he'd never done before, as a big guy anyway. He cried. He couldn't choke back the tears this time.

Whimper. Sniffle. Whimper. Sniffle.

Suddenly, the bushes near him rustled. Max's eyes opened wide, and his tail shot up. "What? Who . . . Who's there?" His voice trembled.

Two yellowish eyes glowed through the bushes. "It's okay, Max." A little dragon, about four feet tall, made his way into the clearing. He was as dark as midnight.

Max tried to get up, but his legs shook beneath him, so he stayed put. "It's you. You're the guy who was in my yard this morning. You're just a kid. And, you're . . . a dragon."

The little dragon inched his way closer to Max. "Yes, I'm Runic. And, I'm sorry for all the trouble I've caused. You're here because of me."

Max scratched his head. He didn't expect to understand this—this dragon from this weird place. Then, he stopped and brought his focus back to Runic. "Okay, it doesn't matter that you brought me here. The important thing is to get me back where I came from."

Runic lowered his eyes then his head. "Well . . . that's going to be a problem."

Max gathered his strength and stood up. "What do you mean, a problem?" he said as calmly as possible. "You got me here. You can get me back. There's no problem. No problem at all. Just get me back." A lump grew in Max's throat as he wondered if he would ever see his mom again.

Runic began to pace. "Well, you see . . . uh . . . I don't really know how I got to your land or how you were able to follow me. What I do know is what I used to get there and back only works once."

"Only once?!" Max's lump disappeared, and he seemed to grow in size he was so mad . . . and scared. His one ear stood straight up. His fur stood up in clumps. "Wait a minute. You're telling me I'm stuck here? You can't get me back? This can't be. NO WAY!"

Runic backed away from Max then darted into a bush.

"Wait! I'm sorry," said Max. "I didn't mean to scare you. It's just that . . . It's just that I miss my home. I miss my yard. I miss my spot by the back door. I miss my toys. I miss my mom and dad. Right about now, Dad would be getting home from work. I'd jump all over him, almost knocking him down. He'd laugh and pet me and tell me I'm a crazy dog. Then he'd call me for dinner. Mom's the greatest, too. I love it there."

SNIFFLE.

"Are you crying *again?*" said Runic through the bushes.

Max shook his head. "I'm NOT crying. Something here is just making my nose itch. I'm three years old. In dog years, I'm a big guy. And, big guys don't cry."

Runic edged his way back to the clearing. "Hey, when you got mad, only one of your ears went up. What's wrong with the other one?"

Max flapped his floppy ear with his paw. "Yeah, I know. This ear only moves when I'm running fast or jumping around. Don't know why. But, let's get back to my problem, please."

"I know," said Runic. "I'm really sorry. We'll figure something out. By the way, it's okay to cry. Even big guys cry when they get hurt or really scared. My dad told me that. And, he's a HUMONGOUS dragon."

Max moved close to Runic and sniffed him. He wanted to get off the "crying" talk. "You sure smell like nothing I've ever smelled before. I'm used to smelling cats and possums and squirrels and other dogs and all sorts of other animals back home. None of them smell anything like you. This whole place smells different than my home. Okay, back to my problem. Let's think this through.

How'd you get to my world? You have to remember something. We'll go over it step-by-step."

# CHAPTER 3

## RUNIC'S MAGIC STONES

R unic rustled his wings and scratched his head. "Let me start from the beginning." He began to pace again. "You see, I have three older brothers, and they're always picking on me. They're allowed to do so many cool things, like fly around without Mom or Dad. Everyone's always telling me I can't do this. I can't do that. I'm not a baby, you know." Runic wrinkled up his face as he talked and showed his mini dragon teeth.

"Anyway," Runic went on, "my mom has these special stones. When she gets them, she hides them, but, I know where. She doesn't know I know, though..."

"Whoa!" Max threw his paws in the air. "I don't want your life story. I just want to know how I got here and how I can get home. Now, regroup and focus."

Runic laughed and with each exhale, a small puff of smoke came out. "Yeah, I have a tendency to blabber on and on. I'll focus now. I promise. Like I said, my mom has these special stones. They're kind of magical. She calls them jewels. They're all different colors, and each color has its own magical power. Like—"

Max put his paw on Runic's shoulder. "Listen. Does this have to do with my problem? I just want to make sure. It's fascinating and all, but I just want to know what's necessary to know. Got it?"

"No. This is all important stuff. It's how I got you here," said Runic.

Max shook his head. "Oh, okay. Go ahead."

Runic found a rock to sit on. "It's kind of late for me. I'm getting tired. Anyway, I was mad this morning, so I took one of my mom's jewels—the clear colored one. I wasn't sure what powers it had. I thought it would make me invisible or maybe strong enough to pick on my brothers."

Max's one ear stood at attention. He might be lost in another world, but Runic's story was getting interesting. "So, tell me already. What power did the clear jewel have?"

Runic lowered his head. "It's one of the most powerful jewels. It seems it can transport the user to other time periods and other worlds."

Max's eyes grew wide. "But, how do the stones work? What do you have to do to get it to work?"

"Well," said Runic, "I'm guessing you think of something while you hold the jewel and it does what you think. When I took the clear stone, I was so mad at my brothers I wished I was somewhere else. Then POOF. I landed in your yard."

Now, Max paced. "Wow. I can't believe this. Magic jewels that can whisssh you anywhere you want. It's crazy. But, you said it only works *once?*" Tilting his head, Max began to wonder. *What if*

*I'm really trapped in this strange dragon world forever? Where would I live? What would I eat? Could I be eaten?* Max shuddered.

"Ahem," said Runic. "It looks like you got lost in your thoughts. To answer your question, it's yes. From what I overheard my mother tell my aunts, each jewel only works once."

The dark night air brought a chill with it. Max was suddenly freezing.

"I've got to get home. My mom and dad will be super mad at me for being out this late," said Runic.

"But . . . but, what about me?" Max's lower lip drooped, and a tear made its way down his cheek.

GAUK. BUAK. GAUK. BUAK.

SCREECCCCHHHH.

GAUK. BUAK. GUAK. BUAK.

Max stood at attention. "Wha-what's that? I heard it before."

Runic jumped up and flapped his wings. "That's Screecher. He's a 10-foot vulture who eats anything he can get a hold of. We've gotta get out of here. If he sees us, we're goners! Follow me!"

Runic darted into nearby overgrown brush and raced as fast as he could. Branches crackled, and leaves crunched as he went deeper and deeper into it. Max galloped after him. It was so dark he couldn't see much of anything. To stay safe, Max made sure he kept his eyes pinned on Runic's tail as the dragon trampled through the woods.

After running a while, they came to a cluster of caves hidden amidst giant trees and more overgrown brush. Runic stopped short. "We're here," he whispered. "Be quiet. We can't let my brothers find you. I don't know what they'd do."

Max's tongue hung from his mouth. His chest heaved up and down. He took a moment to catch his breath. "Oh, boy. So, I have to worry about being lost, about Screecher, and now your brothers?" His one ear flew up like a flag. He didn't like the growing list of scary things.

"Don't worry," said Runic. "It'll be fine. I've gotta go, though."

"But, what about me? I . . . I've never slept outside before. And, what about Screecher or any other wild thing here? I'm too young to be a goner."

Runic scratched his head. "Oh, yeah, right. Follow me." Runic led Max to a small cave at the far end of the cluster. "This is where family stays when they visit. My cousins love it in there. It's got everything you'll need. And, it's got the scent of my father. Nothing will go near it with that scent." Runic gave a big yawn. "You'll be safe. I'll come get you in the morning, and we'll try to figure something out."

Max watched Runic head toward the big cave. Then he was gone. Max had never felt so lonely. He inched his way inside the little cave. Rocks jutted out from the walls. Stones embedded in the rocks gave off enough light so Max could see. As he traveled deeper into the cave, the stones gave off even more light.

He sniffed around with one ear high in the air. "Whew. Runic was sure right. That's a super-strong scent his father has. No wonder nothing comes in here. It smells like burnt leather." Max's nose stung for a couple of minutes until he got used to it.

Going a little further in, Max came to a large opening. A glowing stone rested in the ground in the center of the area. He moved closer and closer to it. "Whoa," he whispered. "It's giving off heat. Runic was right. This place is okay."

Max looked around the cave and found what looked like a waterhole. It was clear and looked fresh. He sniffed it. Once it passed the sniff test, he licked it. "It's okay," he mumbled to himself. He took a few laps of the water then looked around some more. He found blankets on shelves, and there was some kind of food that looked like beef jerky, only lots, lots bigger. These were the size of pizzas.

Seeing the food, Max realized how hungry he was. His stomach confirmed it with lots of rumbles and grumbles.

Max sniffed the food. "Hmm. Smells pretty good." He licked it. Then he took a little bite. He chewed and swallowed. "That's really good. It almost tastes like bacon." He took another and then another. He ended up eating three of them.

After he finished the jerky, he sniffed the water again. He drank and drank and drank.

Next, Max took a couple of blankets and made himself a bed near the glowing stone. He curled up and laid his head down. His mouth opened wide in a big yawn. *Traveling to another dimension, or planet, or whatever the heck this is, is exhausting.* His thoughts went on and on. He thought of Mom and Dad. He thought of his yard and running after possums, squirrels, rabbits, and all sorts of other animals. He thought of sitting by the back door and hearing Mom or Dad call him for breakfast or dinner. Soon, though, his thoughts turned to dreams.

# CHAPTER 4

## STRANGE DANGERS

"Max. Max. Get up." Runic shook Max. Max stretched and rolled over. "Huh?" He opened one eye then the other. "What?"

Runic went back to the cave opening to make sure no one was around. His dark blue scales caught the morning sun. "It's light out. You've got to get out of here before my brothers get up. They're not as big as my dad, but they're pretty big."

Max jumped up. He checked his body. "Yes. Nothing came during the night to take a bite out of me. Do I have time for breakfast?" His belly rumbled and tumbled again.

"I don't know," said Runic impatiently as he scratched the cave floor with his claws. "Maybe just take a few biscuits with you?"

"Biscuits? Those things are biscuits? They're huge. They're the size of a pizza or a loaf of bread." Max grabbed a couple of biscuits and followed Runic out of the cave. "So, what's the plan?" said Max as he gobbled one biscuit down.

Runic didn't answer. He just kept walking. All Max heard was Runic's tail slithering across the dirt.

"Hey, Runic. What's the plan?" Max said louder. He quickened his pace to catch up to the little dragon.

Runic lowered his head and turned to Max. "Okay, I don't have a plan. My mom noticed the clear jewel was missing and questioned me and my brothers. She was really upset. I think that was the only clear jewel she had."

Max furrowed his brow. "Maybe she can get more. If she got it before, she can get it again. Right?"

"Uh, I guess. I don't know. I suppose," Runic crinkled his brow. "But, she doesn't know about *our* problem. She doesn't plan on going for more until she needs to."

"What?" Max's face grew long, and his mouth fell open. "What do you mean? Didn't you tell her I had to get home? You don't know how to get me home. I thought you'd at least ask her for help."

Runic jutted his wings out. "Are you crazy? I can't tell my mom. She'd ground me for the rest of my life. And, if my brothers found out . . . geez. I don't even want to think about that." Runic paced the ground between two giant dragon blood trees. At least that's what they looked like to Max because the leaves were blood red and they were kind of shaped like dragons.

Max gathered his thoughts. "All right. Then we have to come up with a plan. Do you know where your mother gets the jewels from?"

After wearing a track in the soft ground, Runic stopped pacing. "Well, yeah, kind of. There's a really deep cavern far to the north. My mother flies there. But, I can't fly. My wings aren't strong enough yet."

Max narrowed his eyes and tightened his lips. "Then we have to go there somehow and get a clear jewel to get me home. Which way do we go?"

Runic raised his brows. "Uh . . . that's not a good idea."

"Why not?" said Max.

"Cause that's where Screecher and all the other vultures live. And, the cavern is super huge and super deep with a skinny little path leading to a cave at the bottom." Runic spread his wings wide. "If we can get in there, we don't stand much of a chance getting out."

GULP. "But, we don't have a choice." Max's eyes darted back and forth. Then, it came to him. "Hey, didn't you say one of your mother's jewels could make you invisible? And, another can give you super strength?"

Runic's eyes widened. "Yeah, they do special stuff." Then he furrowed his brows, "But, I don't know which stones do what."

Max's one ear bolted up. "Well, we're gonna find out. You've gotta go back home and get one of each jewel."

Runic fluttered his wings and shook his head. "No way. You're crazy. My mother's already on high alert over the jewels. There's no way I can sneak in and get them."

"Okay, okay." Max pulled his mouth to one side then the other. He did this sometimes when deep in thought. "I've got an idea. We'll cause a diversion outside. Everyone will have to run out to look."

Runic tilted his head to one side. "But, what's a diversion?"

Max realized this wasn't going to be easy. "Okay, a diversion is when you do something to draw attention away from what you are really planning on doing."

"Ah," said Runic. "What kind of a diversion are you thinking of?"

The two had walked quite a way from the caves as they talked. Max found a BIG rock to sit on.

"Hmm. I hadn't thought that far," said Max. "Hey, this rock doesn't feel that hard. I never felt a soft rock. This place is crazy."

Runic backed away. "Uh, Max."

Max lifted his leg and licked between his toes. "Yeah?"

"I think you'd better get up. Just do it slowly and walk toward me."

Max stopped grooming himself and looked at Runic. "Why? What's the matter?"

Runic kept walking backward. "Well, you're kind of sitting on one of the deadliest snakes around here. Don't make any sudden moves."

Droplets of sweat began to bead up on Max's forehead. His heart started to hammer away. "A . . . a . . . snnnaaaakkke?" His voice quivered. "I- . . . don't like snakes. I--"

Just then the snake moved. Its tail started shaking. It raised its head, turned, and narrowed its purplish eyes. It glared at Max.

"AAGGGGGGGGHHHHHHHH."

With one swift move, Max dug his hind legs into the snake and leapt toward Runic. He leapt so hard and far; he landed right on top of Runic. The two tumbled and rolled down a hill, thankfully, away from the snake. As they bounced and rolled away, they heard a loud HIISSSSSSSSSSSSS.

Max landed on his head . . . again. *I've really got to stop doing that*, thought Max. Then, Runic tumbled over him and ended up in a ditch.

"Whew. That was a close one," said Max. He rubbed his throbbing head with his paw.

"You have no idea," said Runic. "That snake would have swallowed you whole."

Max stopped rubbing his head. His one ear jutted up. "Whadda ya mean? It didn't look that big," said Max.

"Ha," said Runic. "Most of his body was burrowed in the ground. You only saw about a quarter of him. They stay in the ground to keep cool."

Max shook his body. Fur flew in every direction. "YIKES! Good thing we were near the edge of that hill. This place is sure dangerous. How about warning me if I'm doing something that could get me, well, eaten, or hurt or any other thing that you know I wouldn't like?"

Runic crawled out of the ditch. He looked at Max who had leaves and twigs in all sorts of places all over his body, even in between his paws. Runic held his belly and laughed until he fell back into the ditch. Then Max let out a belly-holding laugh.

"That was pretty hysterical," said Max as he helped Runic up. "You fell right back into the ditch."

"Yeah," said Runic, brushing himself off. You look pretty funny yourself. Okay, let's get back to business. We've gotta think of a diversion plan."

Max pulled the leaves and twigs off then scratched his head. "Yeah, right. We've got to come up with a really good diversion.

If I don't get out of here soon, this place is gonna get me. Are there any other things I should keep my eye out for?"

Runic tilted his head and crinkled his brow. "Hmm. Okay, you know about the vultures and the snakes. There's also the groppers, the killing trees, and some other stuff you've gotta be careful of." Runic took a breath. "Oh, and there's quicksand."

Max's brows shot up so far into his forehead it hurt. And, his eyes opened wide. He looked all around. "Groppers . . . quicksand. Oh boy, this isn't good." Max scratched his head again. "Hey, what's a gropper?"

# CHAPTER 5

# MAX AND RUNIC'S CRAZY PLAN

A shiver went through Runic. "Ohhhh. Groppers are creepy and sneaky. They're really long, kind of like a serpent, but they have arms and legs all along their body. They hide in the bush and even in the sandy areas. And, they creep up on you and grab you. If you're really fast, you can get away. But, if not, first they crush you. Then they eat you."

Max felt an icy chill creep up his spine. His tail stood straight out behind him. His fear was building. There was just too much danger in this . . . whatever the heck land he had accidentally been sucked into.

"Oh, no!" Max said with a quivering voice. "H-How do you avoid them?"

Runic shivered again. "You don't. They're so sneaky you never know when they're around until they're grabbing you. And, they have like a thousand teeth, so once they latch on, you're pretty much a goner."

"Yikes. Another creature I have to worry about. One way or another something's gonna make me a goner if I don't get out of here." Max sniffed the air. "I don't smell anything different. Do they have a smell to them?"

Runic scratched his head. "You know I never took notice. But, now that you mention it, they kind of smell like rotten meat."

"Great! That's an odor I should be able to smell. And, before it's on top of us."

"Okay, already," said Runic. "Will you stop it about the groppers? The only thing you have to remember if one gets you is to get out of its clutches super-quick. We should think about how I'm gonna get those stones from my mom."

"Oh, yeah, right. That's the only way I'll get out of here. We need a plan." Max scratched behind his ear. He lifted his head and let out a long "AGRRRRRRUUUUUU."

Runic's wings waved wildly. "What's that?!"

Max stopped his howling and looked all around. "What?! What are you talking about? What is it?"

Runic threw his wings out wide. "It's you! What was that noise you made? That was scary!"

"Huh. What noise?"

"It's YOU," said Runic. "You made a crazy noise!"

"Oh, you mean my howl?" Max raised his brows into his forehead again and his lips curved up. "So, that startled you? Oh, boy. I have a great idea." He moved his head this way and that. Then he tugged on his floppy ear.

"All right already, what is it? What's the idea?" said Runic.

"It's so simple that it's ridiculously simple. I'm so glad I howled." Max ranted on.

"Max!" yelled Runic. "Just tell me the idea."

"Oh, sorry." Max raised his one ear. "Well, if you were startled by my howl, I bet your family will be, too. That's the plan. I'm gonna howl as loud as I can. When your family runs out of the cave, you run in and get the stones. Pretty good plan, right?"

Runic tightened his lips and narrowed his yellowish eyes. "Uh . . . what happens when my family runs out to find what's making the noise? They're gonna be going after you!"

"Oh, boy." Max raised his brows, and his eyes opened wide. "I didn't think of that. That could be a problem. I'd have to have a really good hiding place. How's their sniffing ability?"

"What do you mean, sniffing ability?" said Runic.

Max put his nose in the air and sniffed around. "I mean can they smell good like me? If I hide, will they be able to smell me and find me?"

Runic tilted his head to the side and thought for a second. "Ah, got ya. No, not as good as you. I'm pretty sure if you hide in the fruit groves they won't find you as long as you don't move or make any noise. We have really good hearing."

Max trotted around. "I can be as still as a mouse and just as quiet. Wait till you see. I once sat for two hours in my yard, really quiet, trying to get a sneaky gopher. He kept digging up my mother's garden, and she was fuming. I figured if I could get him she'd be so happy she'd give me extra treats. I waited and waited and—"

"MAX! Would you please concentrate?" yelled Runic. "I believe you. You can be quiet. Now, how about practicing that?" Runic arched his back. "Geez! You're as bad as me with ranting on and on. Now that we know how we'll get my family out of the cave, we have to decide the best time to do it."

The two friends (yes, over the course of a day and a night, these two wildly different creatures became friends) mulled over this idea and that idea.

"What about early in the morning, when the sun begins to rise?" Max's one ear perked up. "Maybe they'll still be so sleepy they'll be confused, and it'll be easier to fool them."

Runic stretched his wings and puckered his lips. He thought for a moment. "Ya know, that's not a bad idea. My brothers are kind of in a stupor when they first wake up, especially before they eat breakfast. But, my mother and father are pretty much always on the ball. Still, our plan may work. I think with my brothers running around, they'll all be a bit confused and startled."

Max jumped high into the air. Both ears flew up. The floppy one settled back into its usual position. "Yippee! We've got a plan to get me home."

"Hey, not so loud," said Runic. "There are lots of scary things around here. You don't want to bring us to their attention. Not to mention, my brothers are probably roaming around now."

"Oh, yeah, right." Max crouched down a little as he looked around. "Sorry. So, we'll do the diversion in the morning. In the meantime, you have to show me where I can hide after I howl."

Runic brought Max back toward the caves. Right before they came to the clearing, he pointed to the left. "See those short trees over there? That's one of the fruit orchards. The smell is pretty strong, so my family won't be able to find you in there."

Max sniffed the air. "Oh, yeah. I can smell them from here." He followed his nose and investigated the orchard to find a safe spot to hide in the morning. He poked his nose in this hole and that hole. Then he found a hole behind several trees clumped together. And, it was just the right size for him.

Snuggling into the hole, the earth felt cool and, surprisingly to Max, a tiny bit calming. He'd never been in a hole big enough for him to hide in. "Runic, go into the clearing and check if you can see me or smell me."

Runic raced to the clearing. He looked all around the orchard then sniffed around. "I think it'll work! I can't see or smell you." He raced back to Max and spread his wings out wide. "Hey, I forgot about me! How am I going to get in and out without getting caught?"

Max wiggled out of the hole. He shook his body from his head to his tail, and a spray of dirt flew in every direction. "Oh, boy. Let me think a minute." Max paced through the orchard. He raised his head like he had a great idea then lowered it. Max did this a few times, then, finally, he raised his head and kept it up. "I've got it. You'll be inside the cave when I howl. As soon as your family runs out, you zoom into your mom's room and grab the stones. Then zoom out, like you just heard the howl. On your way out, throw the stones behind a tree or something. Oh, better yet, we'll dig a hole at the base of a nearby tree. You can drop them in there on your way out."

"Hey, that's a great idea, Max! Then once the commotion dies down, we can get the jewels. It's brilliant!" Runic flapped his wings so hard; he lifted off the ground, just a bit.

Max smiled, and his big brown eyes lit up. "Yeah, that is a pretty good idea. And, nice lifting."

Runic wobbled his head, feeling a little proud over his newfound ability.

"Now, let's find the perfect spot," said Max. The friends searched around and found it, the perfect spot to dig a hole for the jewels. They went over the plan again and again and again until the sun began to set.

"Okay, Max. I've got to get home. You go back to your cave. I'll see you in the morning after the diversion. Be sure to get up extra early."

"Roger that," said Max.

Runic scratched his head. "Roger? Who's Roger? My name is ROOOO-NIC, remember:"

"I know your name," said Max. "It's a thing from TV."

Runic scratched his head again. "Okay, what's TV?"

Max crunched his brows upward. "That's right. You don't know much about my world. Just like I don't know much about your world."

"That's for sure," said Runic. "The important thing, for now, is don't forget to get up on time." Waving bye, Runic hurried home.

# CHAPTER 6

# SNEAKING THE STONES

When Max went into the cave, he realized he hadn't eaten since breakfast. His stomach made sounds he'd never heard before. Deep, loud rumbles that felt like they came from the very bottom of his stomach. He grabbed a bunch of biscuits and sat near the glowing stone. He ate one after the other until his belly felt full and was poking out. He drank some water to wash down the biscuits then laid down and licked his paws. He closed his eyes on the fluffy pile of blankets.

Max rolled over on his back. He opened his eyes and smiled at Runic.

"MAX!" Max shot up quicker than a jack-in-the-box. "OH, NO. What time is it?"

Runic shook his head. "I figured you'd oversleep. You've got to get out there right now. Just give me a minute to get back in my cave."

"Yeah, yeah. Sure." Max shook the sleepiness off. He watched Runic get back to the cave, then snuck to the fruit orchard. He got into position. He raised his head and let out the loudest and longest howl ever. One he'd never made before.

AGGRRRRRRRUUUUUUUUUUUUUU!!!

He made a mad dash for the hole and jumped in.

From his safe place, Max heard screeches then deafening vibrating rumbles. His ears rattled as he poked his head up just a tiny bit to see. Then he saw them!

First came Runic's dad. At least Max assumed it was his dad. The dragon had to be at least 10 feet tall. His scales were sapphire blue, and he had a white diamond shape emblazoned on his forehead. He flew-ran out of the cave, stood by the entrance and looked all around. His wings stretched out to almost double his body length.

Right on his heels and knocking the first dragon over on his way out was an even bigger dragon. He was at least two feet taller than the first and had bronze-colored scales that picked up every glint of the sun. A green round mark was stamped on his forehead.

Max's eyes grew wider and wider. He was a bit afraid his eyes might fall out of his head they were opened so wide. *Uh, oh. That must be the dad. They're bigger than I thought.* His body shook, and the tip of his lazy ear twitched.

Then came a third dragon, even bigger than the first two. He had to be three to four feet taller than the second dragon. He seemed to be made out of silver-gray armor. A red zig-zag shape was carved into his forehead. Dragon three pushed Dragon Two out of the way. He looked around and lifted his head. Then, he let out a penetrating guttural sound.

GRRRRUUUUUUUGGGGG!!!

Max trembled uncontrollably. His heart thudded in his ears. He used all his might to keep from popping out of his hiding place and running away. Then he heard a steady and slow, THUMP. THUMP. THUMP. THUMP. THUMP.

He gaped at the most humongous, scary creature he'd ever seen before. It looked bigger than his house at home. It had to be 20-25 feet. It thumped its way out of the cave. The emerald green dragon had to lower his head to get out, a gold mark on his forehead glistened in the sunlight. The first three dragons shuffled out of his way.

*Okay, this has got to be Runic's dad. He . . . He's—*

Max's thoughts stopped. The dad dragon lowered his head then raised it high. He let out a bone-rattling, thunderous sound that made Dragon Three's sound a bit wimpy.

GGGGRRRRRRRUUUUUUUUUUGGGGGG
GGGGGG!!!

The earth-shaking sound rippled the bark on
the dragon-whatever-they-were-called trees. And,
a flock of birds that had nested in the fruit
orchard exploded into the sky, screaming as they
roosted atop a mountain cliff nearby.

As fast as he could, Max dug himself further
into the hole. His paws scooped up the soft dirt
and threw it backward between his legs with
scared-out-of-his-wits speed. He poked his head
up just high enough to see over the edge.

Dragon Dad took a huge breath in and
WWWHHHHHHHOOOOOOSSSSSSS. Fire shot
out of his mouth in a burning burst. The flames
almost reached the orchard. Max could feel the
heat. He felt another kind of heat, too . . . a wet
warmth trickling between his hind legs.

"What was it?" asked a voice behind Dragon
Dad. The voice was softer. It didn't have the deep-
guttural sound.

"I don't know. Whatever it was must have high-tailed it out when they heard us," said Dragon Dad.

Dragon Dad moved to the side of the cave entrance, and Max saw a dragon a little smaller than Dragon Two. It was easy to tell, though, that this was a girl dragon. She was much more graceful than Runic's dad and brothers. Her head, sleeker than the others, scoured the area, assessing any danger as she crept forward. This had to be Runic's mom.

"Boys, you go looking around to make sure whatever made that sound is gone." Dragon Mom swished her dazzling tail. Her scales shone of cobalt blue, emerald green, and deep violet. Each one had a silvery tip.

"But, Mom," said Dragon One. "We didn't eat yet. I'm starving."

"Yeah," said Dragon Two. "Can't we eat first then go scouting?" He hung his head and looked woefully at his mother.

Dragon Mom shook her head. "All you boys think of is eating. Oh, all right. But, as soon as you're done, it's scouting time. Understand?"

"Sure, Mom," they said in unison.

Dragon Mom looked around. "Has anyone seen Runic? Where's my baby?! FATHER, WHERE'S RUNIC?!"

Dragon Dad's green and steel-colored eyes searched the area. "I'm sure he's fine."

Max began to sweat. *Where is he? They're going to go looking for him!*

"I'm right here, Mom." Runic scrambled into view from around the side of the cave. "I thought I'd do a little scouting to make sure there was no danger."

Dragon Mom swooped Runic into her arms and held him close. "Oh, honey, you're too little to go scouting on your own. Don't ever do that again. Next time, take Lodan with you."

Runic snuggled into his mom's chest. "Okay, Mom. Sorry, I worried you. I was up super-early and ate already. I'm going down by the waterfalls."

"Oh, I don't know. That noise we heard was very strange. I don't think you should go away from the caves alone. Lodan, go with your brother."

Runic stiffened. "NO! I mean I'm okay."

Dragon Dad nudged Dragon Mom with his snout. "Mother, he's got to grow up. He'll be fine. Let him be."

Dragon Mom let Runic down. "Oh, all right, but be very careful." She put one long claw on Runic's shoulder. "If anything looks suspicious run home."

"Sure, Mom." Runic raced off toward the orchards.

The rest of the clan went back into the cave.

When Max saw the coast was clear, he wiggled his way out of the hole. His legs felt weak and were still shaking. He slumped down into a quivering, wet heap.

"Did you see all that?" cried Runic in a higher pitched voice than usual. "That was a close call!"

Max raised his eyes to see Runic. "Yeah," he whispered. It was a good thing the whole dang dragon family hadn't seen him, because he wasn't sure he could walk, much less run.

Runic furrowed his brow. "What's the matter with you? We have to get the jewels and head to the cavern. We can't waste a minute. My mom will go crazy if I come home late tonight."

With a scrunched-up face, Max shook his head. "Hey, you're used to your family. For me, it was the scariest thing I ever saw. Your brothers are big. But, your father . . . he breathes fire! I thought I was going to get roasted. Or at the very least, toasted. I was so scared I peed myself. I haven't done that since I was a little pup. You gotta give me a minute to get my calm back."

Runic's face lit up. Then he burst into laughter. "You peed yourself! That's hysterical. You're a funny guy." He laughed so hard puffs of steam shot out. He fell to the ground holding his stomach.

"Yeah, yeah. It's hilarious." Max stood up and waited a minute until his legs felt sturdy enough to walk and until Runic's laughter eased off. "Okay, let's get going."

"Hey, did you see how great I was? Cool as could be. They have no idea." Runic folded his wings under and strutted like a rooster. "Sorry, I laughed, but—"

Max's lip curled up into a smile. "I would've done the same thing! And, yeah, you did a good job. Now, let's get those stones. We'll have to test them out along the way."

Runic shook his head. "Nope. We can't do that. Remember I told you they could only be used once?"

Max stiffened his back. "What? Oh, boy. This isn't good."

"Come on," said Runic. "You worry too much."

Max mumbled and grumbled as they went to get the stones. "Yeah, right. Nothing to worry about. We just don't know which stones do what and we're going through a crazy-dangerous place with killing trees, snakes, vultures, quicksand, and oh yeah, groppers." Max shook his head as he walked. "Right, nothing to worry about at all."

# CHAPTER 7

# THE HUNGRY TREES

Runic grabbed the little bag of stones. He peeked inside . . . "One, two, three, four . . ." He stuck his paw in and moved them around . . . "Five. Great, we have five stones."

Max put his paw on Runic's shoulder. "Hey, be careful you don't rip the bag with your claws."

"Always worrying, you are." Runic closed the bag and put it in a pouch he had hanging around his neck. "See, I came prepared. I have a pouch!"

Max nodded and tilted his head. "Yeah, you're a real boy scout."

Runic furrowed his brow. "What's a boy scout?"

"Never mind," said Max. "Which way to the cavern?"

Runic looked around then stuck his skinny, pinkish tongue out.

Max crunched his face into a puzzled knot. "What the heck are you doing? And, did you know your tongue is ripped right down the middle?"

"We have to head north, so I'm feeling which way that is with my tongue. The air is colder in the north. And, my tongue isn't ripped, that's the way it is. It's forked."

"Oh, boy. I'm learning more about you every minute. All right, enough fooling around. Let's get that stone so I can get home."

Max and Runic traveled north for about an hour when they stopped short. In front of them, the trees became tall, dark, and spooky looking. The trees were so big that they blocked out the sunlight and the day became grim and gloomy. Some of the trees were dark green, some were dark brown, and some were dark purple. Their bark didn't look like bark. It looked more like some kind of a skin covering.

The air was thick. Max thought it smelled like the last time he had trapped a skunk and got sprayed in the face with the most horrible smell ever. The two friends stood frozen as strange creature sounds echoed through the tree's branches.

"Uh, oh," whispered Runic.

Max stood alert with his one ear held high. "Whadda ya mean, uh, oh? And, why are you whispering?"

"I think those are the killing trees? I never saw them up close. And, I never went through them. One thing I do know is they can hear. I heard my father telling my brothers one day."

Max narrowed his eyes and let out a low growl.

Runic pushed Max with his wing. "Hey, don't do that. You don't want those trees to know we're here. And, you especially don't want them to get mad at us."

Just then, the branches of the tree directly in front of them started to move. From high above, peering down on them was a prehistoric-looking insect. Max cringed. "That bug is as big as a Doberman. I hope it's not hungry," whispered Max as he shuffled behind Runic.

"Not sure what a Doberman is, but don't worry. They're ugly, but they're vegetarians. Let's try to stay quiet and remain calm," said Runic in a muffled voice.

"Well, maybe we can go around the trees?" said Max, hoping this was an option.

Runic shook his head. "Nope. It would take all day and most of the night to get around them. We're going to have to go through them."

Max plopped down on his hind legs. "Hmm. Do they ever sleep? Maybe we can wait until they're sleeping. I don't mind hanging around until they drop off."

"Nope. That won't work. They take turns sleeping. We've got to do it."

The two walked s-l-o-w-l-y toward the trees. Right before they entered the woods where the trees clustered together like they were lying in wait for the them, they stopped.

Swish. Swish. Swish. Swish. Swish. Swish. Swish. Swish.

Max's ear bolted up. "What's that noise?! Do you hear that?"

Swish. Swish. Swish. Swish. Swish. Swish. Swish. Swish.

"I . . . I don't know," said Runic.

Max looked behind them. He tightened his lips and shook his head. "It's your tail, you, knucklehead."

"Oh, yeah. It swishes back and forth when I'm scared sometimes. Okay, let's go. Now, listen, we have to stick really close. The best thing is to go as fast as we can. Are you ready?"

Max drew his lower lip between his teeth. "Y-Yeah. Uh, first, what happens if one of us gets grabbed?"

"I guess the other one better get out of there as fast as he can. No sense in both of us getting eaten."

"WHAT?!" Max whisper-yelled. "You didn't say they were eating killing trees. Why does everything in this place want to eat me?"

"Come on, Max. We've gotta do it. I got you here. I've got to get you home."

The two friends moved as close to each other as possible. They walked in step into the trees.

"Run," whispered Runic.

Off they raced. Dirt flicked off their feet and paws. Low-hanging branches brushed against them. Just when they saw light beyond the thicket of trees, Max jerked backward.

"AGHHHHHHHHHHHH!"

Runic had just stepped outside the trees into a clearing. He turned when he heard Max. "I'm coming. Don't let them eat you! I've got to get you home!"

Runic shot back into the trees. He ran so fast, he almost flew. A gigantic purple tree had its branches all around Max, keeping him from moving. Max could hardly breathe. The tree's jagged teeth that looked like the edge of a saw were an inch away from piercing Max's skin. Runic jumped on the thickest branch and clawed and clawed and clawed at it. He left deep grooves in the tree's bark or skin, whatever it was.

The tree kept on going, pulling Max closer to its mouth. Max fought as hard as he could to loosen the branches that coiled around him. Runic let out a ferocious roar—one he'd never uttered before—and chomped fiercely into the branches with his razor-sharp teeth.

"EEEEKKKKKKK! EEKKKKKKKKK! EEEEKKKKKKKK!" The tree trembled and let go of Max. It then shriveled up as it cradled its branch to its trunk. It had shrunk to half its size and didn't seem so menacing anymore.

Runic grabbed Max's neck and dragged him out of the trees.

OOOOMMMMMMMMMM. OOOOMMMMMMMMMM.The trees moaned and groaned.

When they got to the clearing, Max sprawled out on the grass. He looked up at Runic. "Why'd ya come back? You could've been killed."

Runic shrugged. "I don't know. I heard you scream and had to help. I couldn't let anything happen to you. You're . . . you're my friend."

Max's eyes crinkled up, and a smile spread across his face, from ear to ear. "Aw, thanks, buddy. You saved my life. I owe you."

"Okay, okay," said Runic. "Let's not get mushy about it. Let's move. We still have a long way to go."

Max wasn't sure, but he thought Runic blushed. His scales turned a purple-blue and his lips almost curved into a smile.

Max got up and threw himself around Runic. Then he licked Runic all over his snout.

"Hey, cut that out, you goofy—hey, what did you say you're called?"

Max stood tall, holding his head high. "I'm a dog. Mom says I'm man's and woman's best friend."

"Okay, dog," repeated Runic. "Alright, you, goofy dog. Let's go."

"You know," said Max, "you've got a pretty fierce roar. I would've been afraid if I wasn't already scared stiff."

Runic seemed to get taller. He almost looked like he was four and a half feet. "I kind of surprised myself with that one. I never roared like that before. But, then again, I never had to save anyone."

"Boy, I sure hope that was the worst of it," said Max.

"Well," said Runic, "we still have the slippery forest to go through. Groppers like to stay in there. And, then there's the sand marshes. That's where the quicksand is. So, maybe not. But if we stick together, we have a chance!"

## CHAPTER 8

# THOSE SLIPPERY GROPPERS

Max and Runic walked and walked until their feet began to drag. Max noticed the trees around them were now burnt orange, and others were a kind of black-red. And, he noticed he was slippin' and slidin'.

"Hey, Runic. Are you having trouble— waaaaaaa!!" Max slipped out of control. His arms flailed and his legs crisscrossed this way and that way.

"WHHHHOOOOOOOAAAAAAAA."

Both Max's ears flew up in the air as he zoomed across the slippery ground.

BAM!

Max went headfirst into one of the trees. He got up dazed then slipped and fell back down. "Ouch." He put his paws on his head. "It's always my head."

To keep from going out of control, Runic dug his claws into the ground as he walked tenderly forward. He rushed to Max. "You okay, buddy?"

"What kind of place is this? I can't even stand up without falling right back down."

"I told you we'd be going through the slippery forest. This is it. You've got to use your claws to keep from doing what you just did."

Max shook his head and tightened his lips. "Great. You couldn't have told me that before?" he grumbled.

Runic's shoulders bopped up and down as he plodded through the muck. He tried his best not to laugh, but a BIG, HA, HA, HA HA, HA, flew out of his mouth. "Sorry, Max." HA, HA, HA. "You looked so funny slipping all over the place. You should've seen your face."

Max stood up and dug his claws into the slimy green, moss-covered ground. "Wait till you do something stupid. I'm gonna laugh my head off."

Rumble. Rumble. Grumble. Grumble.

Max put both his paws on his stomach. "I'm sure hungry. Is there anything to eat around here?"

"You bet there is. The red trees have great tasting pods. And, here and there on the ground, there's stuff to eat." Runic grabbed a couple of dark red pods off a low-hanging tree. He tossed one to Max. "Here ya go. Taste that."

Max caught the pod in his mouth and bit into it. "Yummmm. This tastes like what we call apples, only better." He looked around for more low-hanging branches. Max stuffed as many pods into his mouth that would fit. When he swallowed one mouthful, he'd go for another. Pretty soon, he sat on the ground and fell over. "Whew. I'm so full I can't move. My mother back home always wanted me to eat apples. I'd have one now and then, but they never tasted like these apples. These are can't-stop-eatin-em good."

Runic stood very still and sniffed around. "Uh, Max. Do you smell anything unusual?"

Max licked his paws then sniffed the air. GULP. "I smell rotten meat." Faster than a peregrine falcon swooping down for its prey, Max was up. "Grroowwwwwl." The scent grew stronger from behind him. He jumped up and spun around. A bunch of groppers crept out of the brush. One of them already had its arms and legs all over Runic. Runic's body shook from head to toe. "Runic! Jump out of its grasp. JUMP!"

Runic couldn't move. Now, two groppers were on top of him. All Runic could do was whimper and shake.

Max saw one, two, three, four—six! They just kept coming. He knew he had to act fast but wasn't sure what to do.

BARK. BARK. BARK. BARK. BARK. BARK.

The barking startled the groppers. Max saw his chance. He leapt onto the two that held Runic and pushed them aside. Then he grabbed Runic and jumped as high as a klipspringer. Well, maybe not a klipspringer. Those little African antelopes can jump 25 feet into the air. But, Max did jump at least 10 feet. He landed on a thick branch in an orange tree. His tongue hung out as he panted. "Whew," he whispered, "that was close. We were nearly dinner . . . again."

Max laid Runic on the branch. Runic continued to shake all over. "Runic, buddy. Runic!"

Runic stared at Max, but his eyes were blank. It was kind of like he wasn't there.

Max grabbed Runic by the shoulders and shook him HARD. "RUNIC! You've gotta snap out of it. You've gotta get me home! You promised!"

Runic closed his eyes. His body trembled long and hard. Then, he opened his eyes. He was back! Whatever trance he had been in disappeared.

Max hugged his buddy. "Boy, you almost scared the pods out of me."

Runic's lips curved into a half smile. "You're a funny guy, Max." He sat up and looked down at a sea of groppers beneath them. "Yikes! I would have been a goner if it weren't for you. Thanks. We're even now."

"Yeah, sure. But, we still have a problem. And, it's a big one," said Max. "How are we going to get out of here without getting eaten by those groppers?"

Max and Runic leaned their heads over the branch and watched the groppers slithering on top of each other, their menacing eyes glaring up at them. It looked like they were trying to make a gropper ladder to get up the tree. Max didn't want to wait around to find out if they'd be successful. A chill ran up and down Max's spine. "Boy, they look creepy."

Runic narrowed his eyes and furrowed his brow. "You know, these trees are all connected.

We could go from branch to branch until we're out of the slippery forest."

Max's one ear slowly rose until it pointed straight in the air. "Hmmm. That sounds like a good idea. Are you okay enough to get moving?"

Runic stood up on the branch. "Yeah, I think I'm good to go. Let's get out of here."

The two friends walked and crawled along the branches from tree to tree. It took a while, but they were finally at the end of the slippery forest. Beneath them, the landscape changed drastically. Instead of a lush forest, now a carpet of sand seemed to go on and on.

"Oh, boy," said Max. "No more trees and brush. Now we can see what's around us."

"I don't think so, Max. That sand is full of quicksand, and there may be some groppers hiding in it."

Max shook his head. "What is it with this place? Livin' on the edge? Scares a minute? Isn't there a safe place here at all? Where do you guys go for vacation? The moon?"

Runic laughed. He laughed so hard he almost fell off the branch. "Max, we're used to it. And, don't forget, when I get a little bigger, I'll be able to fly and breathe fire. I won't have to worry about groppers, or snakes, or vultures, or quicksand."

Max's tail wagged. "Oh yeah. I forgot. You'll be one of the things to be feared around here!"

Runic raised his shoulders and spread his wings. "Yep. I sure will be. Come on."

Max and Runic jumped from the branch and landed on the soft sand.

"Now keep a watch out for anything that doesn't look right. It can be tricky getting out of quicksand."

"I hate to break it to you, buddy," Max jabbed Runic in the belly with his paw. "But nothing in this dragon land looks right."

 # CHAPTER 9

# QUICK SINKING

After taking a few steps on the sand, Max jumped up and down. "Ouch. That's hot!"

"Max, don't jump on the sand. You'll let the groppers know we're here and this sand isn't stable. You could cause a sinkhole."

Max shook his head and whispered, "Ouch, ouch, ouch, ouch," as he tried to walk gently on the hot sand.

"Just be careful," said Runic. "If the sand feels extra soft, back up quick."

"Extra soft? What's that? Uh, oh." Max stopped. "Runic, my foot's sinking in the sand . . . RUNIC, my legs are sinking in the sand . . . RUUUUUUNIC!"

Runic backed away. "Don't move, Max. If you can, lay on your stomach or back. But, do it without moving too much. Focus and listen to me."

Max, as easy as he could, moved his legs backward and upward. At the same time, he tilted his chest onto the sand. After a minute of gentle maneuvering, he was on his stomach, kind of floating. "Okay, now what?"

"Just stay there and don't move. I'm going to look for a stick or some twine." Runic raced off.

Max tried to stay very still, but he did move his head to see where Runic was. He couldn't stretch far enough though to see anything. "NO. Don't do that, Runic. It's okay. You don't have to leave to look for anything. Just stay here. I'm not sinking anymore. I'm not sure how to get out, though. Do you think I can swim out?"

Max waited for a reply from Runic.

"Runic, what are you doing? Runic? Runic! RUNIC!" As Max struggled in the quicksand, his hind legs began to sink.

"It's okay, Max. I'm back."

Brown bubbles popped up around Max's rear area.

"What's that?" said Runic.

"Don't ask," said Max. "You got me kind of scared, you know."

"Okay, I get it. Runic closed his eyes and crunched up his face. "Let's get off that topic. I found a skinny tree branch. When you can reach it without stretching too far, grab it. I'll pull you out."

Max saw the branch. He maneuvered himself as gently as he could and grabbed the branch with his paw. Runic pulled and pulled and pulled. When Max could feel solid ground, he clawed his way out.

"WHEW! Thanks, Runic. Okay, now it's two to one. You know, I don't like this place. I mean, I really, REALLY don't like this place. I just want to go home."

Runic's eyes turned a deep amber color as his face grew sad. "I know, Max. I'd be miserable too if I couldn't get home to my family. Don't worry. I'll get you there. Let's go. This time, follow me."

Runic zigzagged this way and that way. Max followed close behind. After a while, they saw the end of the sand and the beginning of a rocky area leading to a steep mountain.

"Oh, boy. I'm glad we're done with the sand. That quicksand is sure scary. I'm glad you knew how to get me out. You really are like a boy scout."

Runic stopped short. "Okay, what's a boy scout? And, don't tell me never mind."

Max wagged his tail. "All right. Back home there are groups of boys who learn how to survive in the wilderness and how to be helpful to others. They're called boy scouts."

"Oh, a boy scout! Cool," said Runic as he flapped his wings. Then a weird expression covered his face. "What's a boy?"

"Never mind," said Max as he laughed. "I'll tell you when we're in the clear."

Runic threw his wings in the air.

"But-"

"Forget the boy scouts for now," interrupted Max. "I'm just glad we didn't run into any groppers. Let's go. I guess we're going over that mountain?"

Runic folded his wings against his back as he eyed the mountain. "Yep, we've got to go over it. The cavern is at the bottom on the other side. It shouldn't be too hard getting up there. It's getting down the other side that'll be a challenge."

Max bounded toward the bottom of the mountain. "Charge!"

"Wait!" yelled Runic. "Those rocks can be loose. Don't race up there!"

Max got about 15 feet up the mountain when the rocks beneath him gave way. "WHOA!" Down went Max. He landed right on his head.

Runic shook his head. "I told you not to do that."

"I was already in my charge. I couldn't stop." Max sat up and rubbed his head. "Boy, it's always my head." He knocked on his head with his paw. "Good thing it's hard."

Runic brushed past Max. "Stop fooling around. Follow me. You have to make sure of your footing. If some stones don't feel safe, go around them."

Stones tumbled down the mountain as Max and Runic climbed higher and higher. They made sure of every step they took.

When they curved around the other side of the mountain, Max couldn't help notice his surroundings. "This is amazing." A powerful waterfall thundered down the mountain beside them. It crashed down into a pool of crystal clear water. Small animals the size of rabbits scampered about. A mother unicorn and her baby nibbled on colorful flowers along the water's edge.

"I would never have thought a place as dangerous and scary as this could also be so beautiful."

Runic didn't say anything, he just pushed some low-hanging branches out of the way and stood on top of the mountain. "We made it."

SWWWWOOOOOSSSSSHHHHH.

A vulture flew past Runic's head. Runic dove back into the trees. Max dove right in after him, thankfully, not on his head this time.

GAUK. BUAK. GAUK. BUAK.

SCREECCCHHHH.

GAUK. BUAK. GUAK. BUAK.

"Stay low, Max. The vultures know we're here."

Max stuck his head out from the bushes. "Oh, no, there are about 10 of them swarming around out there. What are we going to do?"

Runic rustled his wings. "This is a problem. Those vultures can smell us. They can smell really good. Even if we hide behind rocks going down the cliff, they'll know exactly where we are every second."

Max's eyes darted back and forth. "We need another diversion. What about the stones?"

Runic grabbed the pouch hanging around his neck. "Oh, I forgot about them!" He opened the pouch and took out the bag with the five stones. "The only thing is, we don't know which does what. That can cause trouble. Using a stone is how I got you into this mess."

Max's eyes darted back and forth again. "Okay, put the stones away. We're two smart guys. We can come up with our own diversion. They smell us, so we need to disguise our smell."

"Good thinking," said Runic. "There are some jelly trees back there. Vultures don't like that sweet, fresh smell. We can rub it all over ourselves. That should work."

Max and Runic rubbed the jelly leaves all over themselves, from head to toe. They didn't miss a spot. They looked like gooey, gluey monsters when they were done.

SNIFF. SNIFF.

"You don't smell like you," said Max.

SNIFF. SNIFF.

"You don't smell like you either," said Runic. "We should be good to go. Just try to keep out of their view. They have pretty good eyesight, too."

The two friends crept along the ground to the mountaintop clearing. The vultures buzzed around overhead but didn't hone in on them. Trying not to bring any attention to themselves, Max and Runic moved slow and stayed close to the ground. Inch by inch they made their way down the cliff's dangerous, narrow path.

They didn't talk, and they didn't look up. They just kept moving downward. It seemed like it took forever, but then the bottom of the cliff was before them. Finally, they were able to crawl into some brush.

Max's tail wagged and wagged. "We did it!" he whispered. "I can't believe we did it without using the stones."

Runic hadn't told Max, but he'd hurt his leg on a sharp rock going down the cliff. He tried to stand up but couldn't. "UGH. My leg."

Max's tail stood up. "What happened? What can I do to help?"

Runic looked around. "See those leaves over there and that branch?"

Before Runic could say anything else, Max fetched the leaves and branch. "Yeah. Now what?"

Runic took a claw full of mud and put it on his wound. "The mud down here has healing properties." Then he wrapped the leaves over the mud. "This should fix it up quick. In the meantime, I'll use the branch for support."

Max's mouth curled up to one side. "You know, we're a pretty good team."

"Yeah, we are." Runic got up and put the branch under his arm.

Max moved close to him. "Lean on me. It'll be easier."

The two walked the short distance to the mouth of the cavern. It looked dark and menacing.

# CHAPTER 10

# THE CRYSTAL CAVE

"**W**hoa, it's dark in there," said Max as they stepped into the cavern. "Are you sure the stones are in here? Is there another way to get them?"

Runic plopped down on a rock. "Don't worry, Max." He unwrapped his leg. It had already healed. "That mud works great."

Max examined Runic's wounded leg. "Let me see the other one. It must have been your other leg." He looked at Runic's other leg. "That's crazy. Not even a scratch. I gotta take some of that mud home. A badger in my yard is always nipping at me. This stuff will come in handy."

Runic stood up and threw the branch to the side. "This place is magical. Wait till you see inside the cavern. It leads off into lots of caves."

They walked further into the cavern. It went downward with lots of winding paths. The further they went down, the colder it got.

"What's that?" Max's back stiffened, and his tail shot up straight. "There's something glowing over there."

"That's one of the caves. I don't remember which one has the crystals we need, so we'll have to search each one till we find it."

"Do you hear water?" said Max.

"Yeah. There are streams and even rivers down here."

Max and Runic entered the first cave.

Max's eyes opened wide and his breath caught in his chest. "I . . . I've never seen anything so . . . beautiful."

The ceiling of the cave was covered with blue, purple, green, and orange stones. They were almost transparent and seemed to have a light source within them. Gigantic icicles of the colored stones hung down in massive cone shapes that reached all the way down to the ground. On the cave floor, hills of the transparent-colored stones rose into pyramids so high they touched the ceiling.

In the middle of the cave was a large lake that reflected the colors of the stones. Round, smooth pebbles formed a path, and a kind of bridge jutted out over the lake.

Max eyed the cave from one side to the other, and up and down. Its beauty hypnotized him. He stood frozen in place.

"Max! Max! Snap out of it. We have work to do. The stone we need isn't in here." Runic grabbed Max by his flopped ear and pulled him out of the cave.

Max kept trying to look back at the cave as Runic dragged him down another path.

Runic gave Max's ear a hard tug. "Max!"

Max shook his head then his body. "Wow! That place was awesome. But, it's like I couldn't move."

"Yeah," said Runic. "Some of these caves can do that. We have to keep looking for the cave with the clear stones. We don't have time to be mesmerized."

Max shivered. "Boy, it's getting cold. Is it much further? Oh, I see another cave opening. Maybe that's it?"

Max dashed toward the cave. This cave had a stream running through it. HUGE columns of white stone rose from the ground and touched the ceiling. The columns had dripping marks all over them. Some were thicker at the bottom, and some were the same size all around, from top to bottom. The cave walls looked like they were layered, and each layer looked like it had been dripped into place.

"Whoa. This place is amazing. How'd it get like that?"

Runic came up behind Max, "This cavern is full of caves with stalactites and stalagmites. They're formed from water. The stone is turned into minerals, and it creates crazy shapes and cool colors."

Max turned to Runic. "ARUUGGGG? How do you know all that?"

"My dad loves rocks and minerals and caves. He knows all about this stuff and tells me and my brothers."

Max and Runic went further down into the cavern and found several other caves. Each had its own special colored stones and shapes. But, none of them had the stones they needed.

"Are you sure they're down here?" Max sat on a rock and hugged himself. "It's getting too cold. If we don't find them soon, I'm out of here. I don't want to freeze to death."

Runic stood still. "Do you smell that?"

Max got up, stiffened his back and sniffed the air. "What? Not the groppers again? Although, it doesn't smell rotten."

"No, no. It's a smell I remember from when I came here with my mother once. I think the cave with the clear stones had that smell. This way!" Runic raced off down a path.

After a short while, the two stood at the entrance to a huge cave. Light shone all around it and seemed to bounce off the walls and off the crystal-looking icicles that hung from the ceiling.

Runic clapped his wings together. "This is it! We found it!"

Max stepped into the cave.

"NO! DON'T MOVE! The cave is full of booby traps. If you step into the wrong place, holes open up, and you can disappear forever."

GULP! "You could have told me before. What do I do now?"

Runic studied the floor. "Stay still. There are tiny marks on the spots that give in." He moved beside Max then inched in further and further. "Just stay put, Max." Runic turned to make sure Max stayed still. "I know what I'm--"

The ground opened under Runic. "AGGGHHHHHHHHHHHHhhhhh!"

"RUNIC!" Max stared at the opening. "RUNIC!" He didn't know what to do. He didn't know what the markings looked like, so he didn't dare take a step. "RUNIC!" A tear ran down his cheek. Then another and another and another. "R-Runic."

Just then Max saw something rising out of the hole. The hair on his back stood up, and his heart pounded in his chest. It was Runic's head. A second later his body followed.

"RUNIC! Buddy! You're flying!" Max quickly wiped the tears from his eyes. He didn't want Runic to know he was crying . . . again.

Runic flew out of the hole and went to one of the crystal icicles. With all his little dragon strength, he finally yanked a piece off then flew to

Max. "Did you see that?! I was almost gone, but I started flapping my wings, and it worked. I FLEW!" Runic put the stone in the pouch he had around his neck. "Come on. Let's get out of here. Just back up carefully."

Max took a step backward. "Whew, that was sure scary." He turned around and followed Runic. "Hey, slow down!"

Runic flew and Max raced after him. They weaved up this path and that path until they reached the entrance to the cavern.

The sunlight blinded them for a moment. Then a huge shadow blocked the light.

"Screecher!" they both yelled.

# CHAPTER 11

# FLOCK OF SCREECHERS

G AUK. BUAK. GAUK. BUAK. SCREECCCCHHHH.

GAUK. BUAK. GUAK. BUAK.

The vultures screamed in unison.

Screecher and a mob of his buddies flew straight toward Max and Runic. Max grabbed Runic and threw him back into the cavern. Max raised the hair on his back in an attempt to appear bigger.

BARK. BARK. BARK. BARK. Max clawed and bit anything that went near him. Then he felt something hot on his butt. He dove to the side of the cavern entrance and took a quick look behind him. Runic was sputtering fire!

"Watch out, Max!" Runic flew toward the vultures. The flames from his mouth grew bigger and bigger and hotter and hotter.

GAUK. BUAK. GAUK. BUAK.

SCREECCCCHHHH.

GAUK. BUAK. GUAK. BUAK.

"You're scaring them, Runic! You're scaring them! They're running away! Yippee!"

Just then, Runic's flames began to weaken. In a matter of seconds, there were none. Runic's eyes widened. "Uh, oh." Horrified, he watched as the vultures turned and flew straight at him. "AGGGHHHHH!"

Runic zoomed toward the cavern.

SWWWWOOOOOSSSSSHHHHH.

One of the vultures dove after him with its claws ready to snatch Runic.

GAUK. BUAK. GAUK. BUAK.

The vulture just missed Runic's neck, but his claw slashed the rope that held the pouch. Down went the pouch. It fell and became wedged between two big rocks near the entrance to the cavern.

Runic hit the dirt in the cavern and rolled until he smashed against the wall.

"You okay, buddy?" Max ran to help him.

Runic got up and wiggled his wings. He felt his body and bent his knees. "Yeah, I think I'm okay. But, we lost the stones. I don't know how we'll get out of here without them. The vultures don't like going in here, but when they get hungry enough they're gonna come in after us."

Max paced. Runic swished his tail.

Max stopped and looked at Runic. "Okay, are there any jelly trees in here?"

"Nope," said Runic. "They don't grow in caves. If they did, we'd be good to go. That'd be perfect. We could sneak out, and those vultures wouldn't be able to smell us. We'll have to come up with something else. I'm not sure what yet."

"Whoa, Runic," said Max. "You're ranting again."

Runic shook his head. "Oh, sorry."

Max paced again then stopped. "Hey, wait a minute. We're in a cavern with magical stones all over the place."

Runic tilted his head then straightened it. "You're right! Let's go get some stones."

They raced down the closest path and came to a cave they hadn't seen before. It had green sparkly icicles hanging from the ceiling emitting a green glow throughout the cave. A green stream cut through the middle of the cave.

"Hey," said Runic. "I don't remember seeing this type of stone before. Sparkly. Wonder what they do?" He flew to one of the icicles and struggled to break off a small piece. He tossed it to Max. "Here, catch!"

Max stretched as far as he could to catch it. "Whoa!" He jumped, but just missed the stone. It slammed into the cave wall. Immediately, a bright green light blinded Max and Runic.

Runic spun out of control and landed in the stream. Max threw his paws over his eyes.

"I can't see!" yelled Max.

Runic felt his way to the floor of the cave and lifted himself out of the water. "Me either." He rubbed his eyes and blinked repeatedly. "This is bad. This is really bad. I still can't see."

Max crawled toward Runic's voice, feeling his way along the ground. "Ah, there you are." He felt Runic's wing then moved his paw up to Runic's shoulder. "You okay?"

Runic started trembling and lowered his head. "I never should have touched my mother's stones. Now, we're blind. And, the vultures are gonna get us. I'm sorry, Max. This is all my fault."

Max put his arm around Runic. "It's okay, buddy. We'll figure something out." Just then, he saw a glimpse of light. "HEY! I see light!" He blinked and rubbed his eyes. His surroundings began to come into focus. "I can see! I can see!"

Runic raised his head and blinked. Slowly, he saw light. Then, he saw shapes. A few moments after that, he could see clearly. "I CAN SEE, TOO!" He grabbed Max and hugged him. "I'm glad if all of this had to happen, it happened with you. You're a great guy to be with, especially when things go wrong."

A warm feeling rose up in Max. His cheeks felt hot and grew red. "Aw, back at ya buddy. This is some adventure."

GAUK. BUAK. GAUK. BUAK.

GAUK. BUAK. GAUK. BUAK.

Max's back stiffened. "They're coming after us! What'll we do?"

Runic jetted up to the icicles again. He broke two pieces of stone off and flew back to Max. "Here, take this. When the vultures get close, throw the stone at the wall. But, be sure to cover your eyes after you throw it."

They stood at the entrance to the cave. The vultures got closer and closer.

GAUK. BUAK. GAUK. BUAK.

GAUK. BUAK. GAUK. BUAK.

Their sounds echoed and sounded much louder in the cavern. Then they saw them.

"Throw the stone!" screamed Runic.

Max leaned back and with all his strength let the stone fly toward the wall. "COVER YOUR EYES, RUNIC!"

They squeezed their eyes tight and covered them. Max used his paws. Runic used his wings.

SCREECCCHHHH. GAUK. BUAK.

SCREECCCHHHH. GAUK. BUAK.

BANG. BOOM. BAM. BANG. BOOM. BAM.

Max peeked out from under his paw. The vultures slammed against the walls and fell to the ground. "Run, Runic. RUN!"

Max and Runic jetted out of the cavern. Max raced up the cliff and Runic flew. At the top, as they gasped for air, they watched the vultures stumble out of the cavern. They still didn't have their sight back.

"Let's get out of here," said Runic. Instead of flying, he walked with Max down the mountain.

When they got to the bottom, the sun began to fade from view. Runic rustled his wings. "Uh, oh. This isn't good. My mother's gonna have a fit. The whole family will be looking for me."

Max's tail slid between his legs. "Oh, boy. You're right. This isn't good. Your family scares me. And, they're sure to be mad that you're gone because of me."

"Shh." Runic put his claw gently across Max's mouth. "I hear something." He perked up his ears.

FLLAAAAAAPPPPP.

FLLAAAAAAPPPPP.

FLLAAAAAAPPPPP.

FLLAAAAAAPPPPP.

The sky blackened as Runic's family flew overhead.

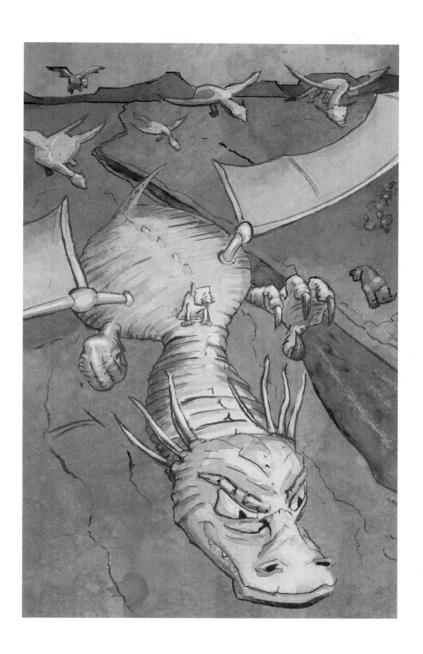

 **CHAPTER 12**

# DRAGON'S EYE VIEW

Max's legs threatened to give out from under him as he watched in horror. His eyes nearly popped out of his head. First, Runic's mother landed beside them. She swooped Runic up and held him close.

Next came the smallest brother. Runic wiggled his head out of his mother's tight hug. "That's Jax," he whispered to Max.

After Jax, the middle-sized brother landed. "That's Lodan," whispered Runic.

Then came, the biggest brother. Smoke puffed out of his nose when he hit the ground. His eyes were blood red with a silver streak down the middle. He used those eyes to glare at Max. Then he moved close and sniffed Max.

"That's Scorch," said Runic. "Don't move and don't look him in the eye. He can be mean."

Suddenly, a strong wind lifted both of Max's ears straight up. Runic's father thudded to the ground. His golden eyes flared. Max could feel the heat from his breath. The rise in temperature actually wilted Max's fur.

Runic squirmed until he got out of his mother's hold. He stood beside Max and looked straight into his father's eyes. "Dad, this is my friend, Max. Max, this is my father, Luchin." Then he looked at his mom. "And, this is my mother, Freya."

Runic's mother moved closer to Max and sniffed him. "Does it fly? Can it breathe fire? What kind of creature is this?"

Runic put his wing around Max. "*It's* my best friend, Mom. Max is really brave! He's a dog."

"Okay, let's go home," said Mother, her lips a little puckered. "We'll discuss all this once we get there. Father, you take Max. Scorch will take Runic."

Runic pumped his chest up, he flapped his wings and stood tall. "I don't need a ride. I can fly! And, I can breathe fire!" He turned his head away from everyone and breathed out a few sputters of fire. After two tries, he got a strong flame going. "See!" he said, wisps of smoke curling from his mouth.

Dad's eyes twinkled.

Mom sighed. "Oh, my baby is growing up."

His brothers smacked him on the head and back. "Way to go, Runi."

"Okay, boys, that's enough. Let's go," said their mother in a gentle, yet firm tone.

Max couldn't help it. He peed himself as Luchin grabbed him by the neck.

Luchin threw Max on his scaly back. "Hold on tight," he ordered in the gruffest, lowest voice Max had ever heard.

Max dug his claws on all four paws into Luchin's back. Massive scales on Luchin's back rose up to help secure Max. The dragon took off with such force, Max's ears were pinned back as was every strand of fur on his body. The air whooshed past Max's ears, muffling out all other sounds. They soared above the magnificent and dangerous land.

Clutching the massive beast's back, Max peered down at the ground. "WHAAAAOOOOO!" He shut his eyes tight then opened them just a bit.

In the distance, Max saw a white river that glistened like melted diamonds. Next to the river, was a herd of some kind of large feathered animal. There were other herds of strange animals that spotted the ground below. In the sky in front of him were three moons just coming into view. It gave Max another perspective of this crazy land.

As scared as Max was, after a while, he felt kind of safe. He had a personal ride from the biggest, scariest thing in this world. He was able to unclench his muscles. The knot in his stomach from struggling to stay alive all day started to dissolve.

Watching the landscape spread out before him, Max's thoughts soared home. He missed his mom. Exhausted, he fought to hold back tears. *What will I do if I can never go home?*

Leading the family back to the cave, Luchin's enormous wings shifted, and they headed downward.

It had taken Max and Runic hours to get to the mountain, but coming home seemed like a short time.

Max was relieved when Luchin landed in the clearing by the cave. It took a minute for Max to release his grip on Luchin's back. His claws were stuck in place, even though he had thought he'd relaxed. Once he let go, Luchin's raised scales flattened out. Max slid down the dragon's back, then jumped to the ground, sending up a soft poof of dirt.

Max fell and tumbled to the center of the clearing. When he looked up, all five dragons surrounded him. "Oh, boy," he whispered. Then he saw Runic flapping wildly to the ground.

"Whew, that was a long ride. I didn't think I'd make it." Runic saw the frightened look on Max's face. He gave his family a hard gaze. "What's going on?"

Freya nudged Max with her nose. "I've never seen such a creature. Where are you from, Max?"

Looking at the ground, Max whispered, "I'm from . . . Earth."

Runic covered Max's back with his wing. "This is all my fault. I brought Max here." He looked at his mother then dropped his eyes to the ground. "I used one of your stones. I was so mad at Jax and

Lodan and Scorch that I wanted to get away from them. So, I took the clear stone and before I knew it, I was in Max's world. He saw me and chased me. Then he followed me through the *hole* back here. We've been trying to get him home ever since."

Max straightened himself up. "It's not all his fault, Mrs. Dragon. I shouldn't have followed him here. And, I kept telling him he had to get me home. I kind of *made* him do it."

"Yeah, but, I brought you here," said Runic. "And, Mom! Max saved my life on our trip to the caverns. More than once."

Max looked at Runic as the corners of his mouth turned up and smiled. "Yeah, but you saved my life more than once, too."

Luchin stomped his foot, and smoke rolled out of his nose. "Enough!" he thundered. "You could have been hurt or worse traveling to the caverns alone. You should know better, Runic. You're punished." He turned his gaze to Max. "And, as for you—"

"Dear," said Freya. "I think Max and Runic have been through quite an ordeal. Maybe we can decide what to do after dinner."

"Alright, Mother. But, I'm not going to forget about this." Luchin stomped off toward the cave. Every step he took felt like it would split the ground wide open, at least to Max. The stomping made Max shake and that jolted him. He realized how close he had come to being eaten numerous times throughout the day. A chill shot through him, from his head to the tip of his tail.

The brothers smelled Max's fear. They stared at him with a mixture of curiosity and annoyance, but mostly annoyance. Their lips curled up over their sharp whitish teeth. Expelling a shaft of steam, Freya motioned for everyone to follow her into the cave.

# CHAPTER 13

## SLUMBER PARTY PALS

At the dinner table, Max's mouth watered when he saw his favorite jumbo biscuits. He and Runic ranted on and on about every detail of their journey. They paused here and there to put food in their mouths, chew it, and swallow. There were giggles and even some laughs as they told about the other's misadventures. Oh, and they paused to breathe now and then.

Luchin and Scorch narrowed their eyes as they listened. Lodan's eyes were opened wide. And, Jax's brows were up in his forehead. Freya shook her head and gasped a few times.

When Max and Runic finished telling everything that had happened, Freya got up. She paced the floor a few times then she sat down. "You two did something very dangerous and foolish. But, you also showed great strength and bravery. Runic, why didn't you just come to me and tell me what happened? I would have helped and so would your father and brothers."

The brothers mumbled under their breath.

"BOYS! Not another sound." Freya shot them a narrow-eyed glare.

Luchin sat with his wings folded and his jaw set tight.

"Mom, I'm sorry I caused so much trouble," said Runic in a hoarse dragon voice from breathing fire for the first time ever. "I knew I did wrong and was afraid of telling you. I know now I should have. But, what's really important right now is we need to go back to the cavern to get the clear stone to get Max home."

Max let out a slow, low whimper.

"What's the matter, Max?" said Runic.

Max lowered his head. "I really want to go home. I miss my family. But, I'm going to miss you. You . . . you're . . . I never had a best friend before."

Runic's lip quivered. "I know. I don't want you to go. But, your family will miss you if you don't."

Max raised his head. He was puzzled as he watched Freya's face brighten.

"Okay, boys. I have a solution to this problem. First, I want you to promise that you will never do anything dangerous again," said Freya in a soft but serious tone.

"Never again," Max and Runic said in unison.

Freya glanced at Luchin. "Is it okay, dear, if I handle it this time?"

Max thought he saw Freya wink at Luchin.

Luchin studied his wife. "Okay."

*Ah*, thought Max, *maybe I won't be dragon toast after all.*

Freya smiled at Luchin. "Thank you, dear. Now, you two. Because you both risked your lives for each other, you are bound together for life. This type of bond will not be broken. Max, I have a special indigo stone for you. It will allow you to come back and forth between our worlds."

Max jumped out of his seat. His arms and ears flailed about. "YIPPEE! This is super-great. It's STUPENDOUS!" He grabbed Runic and danced around the cave. "Thank you, thank you, thank you!"

Runic pulled away from Max as his brothers eyed them.

"He's still a baby," said Scorch.

Max looked Scorch in the eye. "A baby?! Ha! This guy is a hero. He's 10 times the dragon you'll ever be!"

Runic grabbed Max. "Back off, Max. He's just a jerk."

"Jerk or no jerk," said Max. "He can't talk about my best friend like that." GROOWWWWL.

Scorch straightened up and took a breath in. His eyes peeked out from narrowed slits.

"SCORCH! Don't do it," said Luchin as he got up, towering over his son.

"But, he—"

"No, buts. Start controlling your temper!"

"Yes, Dad." Scorch sunk back in his seat.

As this was going on, Freya left the room. A minute later she came back with the indigo stone and a pouch. She put the stone in the pouch and handed it to Max. "Keep it in the pouch until you want to use it. While I know you can go between our worlds with the stone, I'm not sure what powers it will have in your world or how powerful it will be. So, be very careful with it. To test it out at home, just put one of your claws on it. Don't put it in your paw to test it."

Max lifted the pouch. He held it in front of him and stared at it. "Thank you, Mrs. Dragon." He looked at Runic. "I don't want to go, but I know my family is worried sick about me. I don't want to keep them worrying. I-I guess I'll go now."

Max knew from the funny look Runic had on his face that he was holding back tears. He didn't want to cry in front of his brothers.

"You're right," said Runic.

Freya laughed softly. "I should have told you, Max. With this stone, your family won't realize you're missing. What could be days here will seem like minutes to your family."

Max's one ear shot up, and his eyes twinkled. His tail wagged so hard it made a swishing sound. "YIPPEE! I can spend the night. This is GREAT! I'll go home in the morning."

"YIPPEE!" shouted Runic. He tightened his lips and looked at his brothers. "You can call me whatever you want. I don't care. My best friend can stay a little longer. And, even better, he can come back! Come on, buddy. I'll show you my room."

The two pals knuckle bumped then burst out laughing on their way to Runic's room.

Max's stomach began to ache from all the laughing . . . and all the biscuits he ate at dinner.

"Hey, Runic. What is this place called anyway?"

"This is Vaengaria."

Max wagged his tail. "Cool."

Runic wagged his tail, too.

They talked and laughed some more, right through the night.

# ONE UP MAX VIP

Would you like to join the VIP List and find out about the next book coming out in the Adventures of One Up Max series, and also check out special giveaways and events?

Would you like to book the author, Lisa Shawver, (and One Up Max) for a presentation?

Or would you like to find out more about sponsorships and special volume ordering?

You can get more info on ALL of these things and more by simply visiting our special VIP site.

## www.OneUpMaxVIP.com

# ABOUT THE AUTHOR

**Lisa Shawver** is a former middle school administrator and has been a teacher for over 17 years at the elementary and middle school levels and is currently teaching at-risk high school students.

One of her noteworthy accomplishments is competing in softball in the 1996 Olympics. Her inspiration for writing children's books comes from her dog Max and her husband.

She enjoys sharing real-life adventures of Max on social media and creating new adventures for Max and Runic.

*Runic and The Crystal Cave* is her first book and is the first in the One Up Max Adventure series. Watch for more coming soon.

Connect with Lisa on:

Facebook.com/oneupmax/
Instagram.com/oneupmax/
OneUpMax.com

Made in the USA
San Bernardino, CA
05 March 2019